LULU
AND THE FLYING BABIES

FOR:
Tim, Mike, Annie, Clare,
Lucy, Douglas, Juliet,
James, Anna and Rupert.

A RED FOX BOOK 0 09 945115 8

First published in Great Britain by Jonathan Cape,
an imprint of Random House Children's Books

Jonathan Cape edition published 1988
Red Fox edition published 2003

1 3 5 7 9 10 8 6 4 2

Red Fox Books are published by Random House Children's Books,
61–63 Uxbridge Road, London W5 5SA,
a division of The Random House Group Ltd,
in Australia by Random House Australia (Pty) Ltd,
20 Alfred Street, Milsons Point, Sydney, NSW 2061, Australia,
in New Zealand by Random House New Zealand Ltd,
18 Poland Road, Glenfield, Auckland 10, New Zealand,
and in South Africa by Random House (Pty) Ltd,
Endulini, 5A Jubilee Road, Parktown 2193, South Africa

THE RANDOM HOUSE GROUP Limited Reg. No. 954009
www.kidsatrandomhouse.co.uk

A CIP catalogue record for this book is available from the British Library.

Printed in Hong Kong

LULU
AND THE FLYING BABIES

POSY SIMMONDS

RED FOX

I was angry at home....

Ow... **when** are we going to the **PARK**?!

Just hold on, Lulu!

We're getting Willy ready...

Owh!

It's cold... he'll need his hat.

Ooh, yes...

There we are!

Owhh!

COME ON!!

Lulu!

Stop shouting....
...at **ONCE!**

I was angry in the street....

I was angry in the park...

I shouted in the museum....

And when you feel better...

...you come and find us by the dinosaur over there...see...

We rolled in the snow.....

We splashed in the sea....

We growled at a tiger.....

We patted a King....and gave crisps to his horse.....

We ate some cherries......   ...and apples and plums...

...and we spat out the stones down a mountain side....

We got lost in a dark, scary wood.

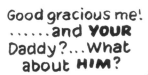

I hugged my Dad and kissed my baby brother...

...**we patted** a **king!** We spat plum stones down a mountain...we got lost in a dark, scary wood. ...we....

Well I never!

Picture books by Posy Simmonds

FRED

LULU AND THE CHOCOLATE WEDDING

BOUNCING BUFFALO

F-FREEZING ABC

LAVENDER